Disney's
My Very First Winnie the Pooh™

Pooh
Welcomes Winter

Written by
Kathleen W. Zoehfeld

Illustrated by
Robbin Cuddy

SCHOLASTIC INC.

New York Toronto London Auckland Sydney
Mexico City New Delhi Hong Kong Buenos Aires

First published by Disney Press, New York, NY.
This edition published by Scholastic Inc., 90 Old Sherman Turnpike, Danbury, CT 06816
by arrangement with Disney Licensed Publishing.

ISBN 0-7172-8868-4

Printed in the U.S.A.

"Winter will be here soon," said Winnie the Pooh. "That's what Christopher Robin says."

"Who's Winter?" asked Piglet.

"The someone who is coming soon," said Pooh.

"Oh, a visitor!" said Piglet. "We should do something nice for him."

"We could give a party," said Pooh.

"What a grand idea," said Piglet.

"Come on," said Pooh. "Let's go tell the others."

Outside, the cold wind was busy blowing the last leaf off the old oak tree. A few fluffy snowflakes flew around in little circles. They rushed down Pooh's collar and settled behind Piglet's ears.

"Maybe we should wear our hats and scarves," said Pooh.

Piglet rubbed his ears. "P-P-Pooh," he chattered, "p-p-perhaps we should stay home now and tell everyone about the p-p-party tomorrow."

"But the party will be over by then," said Pooh.

Pooh put on a hat and scarf. He wrapped a Pooh-sized scarf around little Piglet twice.

By the time they got to Kanga's house, they were so chilled they had to stay for tea.

When they were finally warm enough to remember why they were there, Pooh said, "Winter is coming soon, and we're giving him a party."

"Oh, boy! A party!" cried Tigger.

"Let's go!" cried Roo.

They opened the door. A pile of snow swooshed in and buried them. The wind was quiet. The Hundred-Acre Wood seemed to be napping under a blanket of white. Piglet and Pooh, Tigger and Roo were under a white blanket, too.

They blinked.

"How will we get to the party?" asked Piglet. "The snow's so deep!"

"Don't worry, little buddy," said Tigger, "we'll go by sled!"

Tigger and Pooh pulled. Piglet and Roo rode. Roo reached over the side and grabbed snow to make snowballs. He piled them on the sled.

"These will make good presents for Winter," he said.

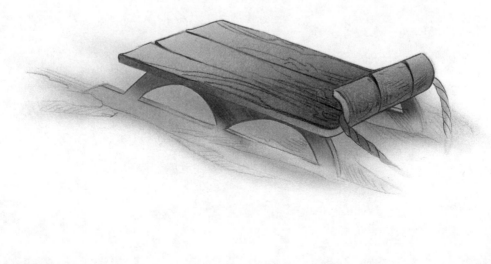

"Winter has arrived!" declared Owl, who had landed on a branch overhead. "I heard Christopher Robin say so."

"Oh!" cried Pooh. "Do you know where Winter is?"

"I haven't seen him myself," said Owl.

"We'll have to hurry and find him," said Pooh. He told Owl about the party. "Would you fly over and tell Rabbit and Gopher?"

"Don't forget Eeyore," whispered Piglet.

"And Eeyore," said Pooh.

"I'd be happy to oblige," said Owl.

As Owl flew off, Tigger and Pooh climbed on the sled with Piglet and Roo.

"Yaaay!" they all shouted as they slid down the hill toward Christopher Robin's house to ask him where they could find Winter.

"There's Christopher Robin!" cried Roo. Pooh called out, "Halloo!"

Christopher Robin didn't answer.

"Oh, no!" cried Piglet. "Maybe he's frozen in the cold!"

"That's not Christopher Robin," said Tigger. "That's Winter!"

"Winter?" whispered Pooh. "How do you know?"

"Tiggers always know Winter when they see him. That big white face—that carroty nose. Who else could he be?"

"Well," said Pooh, "he looks shy. We should be extra friendly." He stumped right up to Winter. "How do you do?" he said. He shook Winter's stick hand. "I'm Pooh, and this is Tigger and Piglet and Roo."

Winter was very quiet.

Piglet nudged Pooh. "Tell him about
the party."

"What party?" asked Pooh.

"You know," whispered Piglet, "HIS party."

"Oh, yes," said Pooh. "We are so happy to
have you in the Hundred-Acre Wood, we are
giving a party in your honor."

Winter did not say anything.

"Oh d-dear," said Piglet. "He's frozen!"

"Quick!" said Tigger. "We
better get him to the party and
warm him up."

They hoisted Winter onto
the sled.

Roo showed him the snowballs. "I made these just for you," he said.

Winter did not even look.

"Wow, he's in bad shape," said Tigger.

Tigger and Pooh pulled. Roo and Piglet pushed. When they finally slid up to Pooh's house, the others were already there. Owl had hung a big friendly sign over Pooh's door:

WELCOME WINTUR

Eeyore had stuck a pine branch in the snow. Little icicles sparkled on its leaves. Rabbit and Gopher were inside making hot cocoa and honey-carrot cake.

Pooh and Tigger wrestled Winter off the sled.

"Give him the comfy chair by the fire!" ordered Rabbit. "Get him some hot cocoa!"

Everyone fussed over Winter. Still, he did not say a word. His carrot nose drooped. His stick hands fell.

"Oh, my!" cried Piglet.

"Maybe he's not the party type," said Eeyore.

"Our cocoa'sss making him sssick," whistled Gopher.

"What are we going to do?" cried Rabbit.

J ust then Christopher Robin tromped up to the door in his big boots.

"Has anyone seen my snowman?" he asked.

"No," said Pooh glumly, "but maybe you can help us. We brought Winter here for a special party, but he doesn't seem to like it."

"Silly old bear," laughed Christopher Robin. "Winter is not a who, it's a what."

"What?" asked Pooh.

"This is my snowman," said Christopher Robin.

"He's not Winter?" asked Pooh.

"No," said Christopher Robin. "Winter is the season—you know, the time of year. Cold snow and mistletoe . . . warm fires and good friends. . . ."

Pooh scratched his nose thoughtfully. "Yes, I see now," he said. "Of course. I am a bear of no brain at all."

"You're the best bear in all the world," laughed Christopher Robin. "Come on, we'd better get the snowman back outside before he melts."

"Oh d-dear," said Piglet. "I hope we haven't ruined him."

"Snowmen are easy to fix," said Christopher Robin. They undrooped the snowman's nose and stuck his stick hands back in.

Eeyore laid the pine branch in his hands. "Well, so much for the party," he said.

"Yes," sighed Pooh. "Too bad."

"Pooh," said Christopher Robin, "we can still have a party to celebrate winter. It's a grand idea!"

"It is?" asked Pooh.

"Sure," said Christopher Robin. "Let's have fun!"

They threw Roo's snowballs. They took turns riding on Tigger's sled. They made snow angels. They caught snowflakes on their tongues. They sang songs and danced around the snowman until they couldn't dance any more.

"Everyone in for honey-carrot cake and hot cocoa!" called Rabbit. They all gathered around the fire.

Christopher Robin gave Pooh a little hug. "Happy winter, Pooh," he said.

"Happy winter!" cried Pooh.